Planted

"Grandpop!" I called out. "Come look at my feet!"

Grandpop examined the bottom of my toes.

"Those aren't what I think they are, are they?"

"They sure are." Grandpop was smiling. "You're sprouting roots, boy."

"What if I had stayed in the mud a little longer? Would they have taken hold? Would I have to spend the rest of my life in the garden?"

Grandpop didn't answer. He just began to chuckle. . . .

Top Secret

by John Reynolds Gardiner

Illustrated by Marc Simont

For Kyle,

John R. Gardiner

A BANTAM SKYLARK BOOK®
NEW YORK · TORONTO · LONDON · SYDNEY · AUCKLAND

To the ideas of tomorrow . . .

Acknowledgments

I would like to pay credit to Andrew J. Galambos for the many ideas and concepts of his, based on his theory of primary property and the science of volition, that appear in this book.

I would like to express my gratitude to my father, Glenn Gardiner, and his sense of humor, which is so much a part of me. I am also grateful to Elizabeth Isele and the staff at Little, Brown, for their enthusiastic support and direction; to Barbara Fenton for her help in developing the story; to Jane Penderghast-O'Reilly for her help in marketing the story; and to Gloria, my lovely wife and loyal partner, whose zest for life is an inspiration to my work.

And to Bob Hudson, Martin Tahse, Sylvia Hirsch, Wells Root, Sy Gomberg, and Ken Gardiner.

Contents

Prologue

I'm writing this down in case something should happen to me.

My name is Allen Brewster. I'm nine years old. I live at 4152 Via Solano. It's the big two-story house. The one with the tile roof.

Today is Saturday, June twentieth, two weeks after school let out for the summer. The time is ten-thirty at night.

There's a brown car parked outside in the street with two men in it. They're watching the house. I have the lights off in my room to make them think I'm asleep. I'm really under the covers writing this down in the back of my old science notebook. I better hurry because the batteries in my flashlight won't last forever, and I have a lot to tell.

My story begins several months ago in Miss Green's science class at school. . . .

Top Secret

1.

Miss Green

It was the day we had to tell Miss Green what our science projects were going to be. I was excited because I had thought of something really neat.

You see, Miss Green made a big deal out of these science projects. At the end of the year there was a Science Fair and schools from all over the country were represented. There were awards and prizes and a *silver trophy* for the best project.

There was also an award for the best science teacher — an award Miss Green had never won. But she wanted to. That's why your science project was more important than your homework or even your test scores. Last year, Miss Green had actually flunked two kids because their projects weren't good enough.

* * *

"Come to order," came the sound of Miss Green's deep voice, and there was instant quiet in the room.

Miss Green stood facing the class, her hands on her hips, her mouth curved downward into a frown. She was a big woman with a large head and a large lower lip that curled up like a bulldog's.

"Let's start with you, Peggy."

Miss Green had written each student's name on the blackboard in alphabetical order, starting with Peggy Applegate.

I was next.

"Ant farm," said Peggy who was sitting right in front of me.

"Stand up when you address me!"

Peggy shot to her feet, her pigtails swaying. "I'm sorry. I forgot." She took a deep breath. "I want to do an ant farm for my science project, if that's all right?"

Miss Green grumbled. "In my twenty years of teaching there has never been a year without an ant farm. Why should this year be any different?"

As she walked to the blackboard, the tractor-tread soles of her shoes made squishy sounds on the slick linoleum floor. "Where are all the thinkers of tomorrow? The scientists? The engineers? They had to be kids once, didn't they?"

She picked up a stick of chalk with her thick fingers. "How I've longed to find a student in my class with an original idea. Someone who showed real imagination. Just one. That isn't too much to ask, is it?"

Miss Green wrote the words ANT FARM on the blackboard in large capital letters next to Peggy's name.

"Allen Brewster," came the sound of my name in a voice that sounded more like a bark than speech.

My heart began to pound against my chest as I stood up. I noticed everyone in the class was looking at me. I couldn't wait to tell Miss Green about my project. She had said she wanted something original. Well, she was going to get it.

"I have an idea," I said, "that's going to win the *silver trophy*."

Everyone in the class started laughing.

Peggy Applegate twisted around in her seat and was grinning at me with a mouthful of braces. Barry Cramer, who sits right behind me, and is the toughest kid in the fourth grade, started kicking my chair.

Even Miss Green looked as if she were about to laugh. "The silver trophy?" she said. "Now really, Allen. You know as well as I do that the silver trophy is usually won by a senior in high school. No one in grammar school has ever won it."

"A kid in the tenth grade won it one year."

"Yes," agreed Miss Green. "But, Allen, he was a genius."

"So, maybe I am too," I said.

Everyone laughed again.

"Believe me, Allen," said Miss Green. "I can think of nothing I would like better than to have you win the silver trophy. But we must be realistic. Wanting to, and being able to, are two different things."

"Don't you even want to know what my idea is?"

"Of course," replied Miss Green, looking over my head at the clock in the back of the room. "But don't take too much time. We still have to hear from everyone else."

I was sure as soon as Miss Green heard what I wanted to do, she would change her mind.

"I'm going to do my project on *human photosynthesis*," I told her.

Miss Green said nothing. She just looked at me.

"I got the idea last night at dinner," I explained. "My mom fixes liver every Thursday. I can't stand liver. And then it just sort of hit me. Plants don't have to eat, right? So why do humans? Why can't we get our food directly from the sun the way plants do?"

"Are you saying sunlight would be our food?"

"Yes. And a little water."

"This is your brilliant idea? The one that's going to win the silver trophy?"

"Yes. You won't find a project more original than that at the Science Fair. I'm sure of it. And you know what, Miss Green? You'll probably win best science teacher because my idea is so good."

Miss Green seemed totally lost for words. She rubbed her face with both her hands for a long time. When she finally looked at me her eyes were red. "That is beyond a doubt the most ridiculous idea for a science project I have ever heard in my entire life."

"Why? You said you wanted something original."

"First of all," said Miss Green. "The mystery of *plant* photosynthesis, the process by which plants convert sunlight into food, has only recently been discovered, and is still not fully understood in every detail."

"That's why I want to do it."

"And, secondly, to adapt photosynthesis to humans is impossible."

"Why?"

"It just is."

"But why? There must be a reason. You just don't know what it is."

Miss Green's eyes narrowed into razor blades. "There's one thing I do know, Allen Brewster. You were told to have an idea for a project by today. You obviously didn't do your assignment."

"That's not true!"

"So, let me tell you what I'm going to do. Since you couldn't think of anything, I'm going to think of a project for you."

She walked to the blackboard, picked up the chalk, and wrote one word to the right of my name: LIP-STICK.

"You will do your project on lipstick, Allen," Miss Green said. "And if it's not the best project on lipstick I've ever seen, I'll flunk you so fast your head will spin."

"But what about human photosynthesis?"

"Assuming it were possible, which it isn't, it would take a genius. And believe me, Allen Brewster, a genius you are not."

2.
Allen

I was mad. Miss Green was not being fair. I did have a project. She just didn't like it.

As I rode home on the bus, I made up my mind that I was not, under any circumstances, going to do my project on lipstick. I would solve the mystery of photosynthesis, and I would adapt it to people, just like I said I would.

I closed my eyes and visualized the Science Fair. I could see the silver trophy, and all the kids at school gathered around my project. I could see Miss Green apologizing to me for ever having doubted my ability. And there was Peggy Applegate. And Barry Cramer . . .

Barry Cramer! I *could* see him. I could see him in

the rear view mirror over Ivan's head. Ivan's our bus driver, and I was sitting right behind him.

I kept my eyes on the rear view mirror as Barry slowly made his way up the aisle toward me. He was crouched real low, trying to stay out of sight.

And then I saw it — in his hand. He had a thing of lipstick. I wasn't sure what he was planning to do, but whatever it was, I knew I wouldn't like it.

I had to think of something. And fast.

And then I got a terrific idea. The only problem was that my timing would have to be perfect.

Continuing to watch Barry out of the corner of my eye, I inched my way forward to the edge of my seat. He was almost to me now. I could see him fumbling with the top of the lipstick. I could see his hand reaching out toward my neck.

Now! I stood up, stuck my finger in my mouth, then ran my wet finger along the back of Ivan's neck and sat back down. The whole think took no more than two seconds.

"Hey. . . !" growled Ivan, looking into the rear view mirror and right into the face of Barry Cramer, who was holding the lipstick.

Barry got thrown off the bus. He would have a long, long walk home. Everyone laughed and whistled at him.

"Just wait!" Barry shouted at me, shaking his fist.
"I'm not afraid of you," I shouted back, feeling
extremely brave as the doors closed in Barry's face
and the bus took off. I knew I wouldn't stand a
chance against Barry Cramer. He was at least one

year older and a lot bigger than I was. He was held back last year because Miss Green hadn't liked his science project.

The bus let me out about a half a block from my house.

"It's just me, Lampchop," I yelled to our dog as I walked up the walkway to our front door. Lambchop had started barking. She can't see too well. I put some glasses on her with a rubber band once, but they didn't help.

Our cat, Waffle, was waiting for me on the front porch with his arms and legs outstretched. I knelt down and petted his stomach, careful to pull my hand away as he started to bite. Cat's weird.

I walked around to the backyard, looking for my grandfather. I had to tell him about Miss Green.

"Hi, Grandpop!" I called out when I saw him. Grandpop was on his knees examining some strawberry plants. He was wearing tennis shoes with no socks, and a straw hat that covered up most of his white hair.

"Would you look at this?" he said in his soft voice, holding the tiny leaf of the strawberry plant in his hand. "See that little critter?"

Grandpop has the shakes, so I held his hand to

stop the leaf from moving and looked real hard. All I could see was a tiny little dot on the leaf. "You mean that dot?"

"That's a mite," said Grandpop. "Darn parasite if there ever was one." Then he looked at me with his watery blue eyes. "I saw a photograph of a flea once, magnified many times, and you know what was on its neck?"

"No," I answered. "What?"

"A mite." Grandpop rubbed his chin. "And then I got to thinking, what was on the neck of that darn mite?"

"Was there anything?"

"I don't know. But if there was, do you know what I'd be wondering about next?"

"What was on the neck of the thing that was on the neck of the mite?"

"You got it," said Grandpop, smiling.

"I never thought about that before," I told him.

"Always think about things, Allen." Grandpop pointed a skinny finger at me. "Cause you know what you are when you stop thinking, don't you?"

"What?"

"You're dead."

My mother opened the back door and called to

me through the screen. "Allen, time to set the table. Your father will be home any minute."

"Okay, mom, coming," I yelled back. "Talk to you later, Grandpop."

I walked in the back door, careful not to let the screen door bang. The house smelled of fried chicken. Sure beats liver, I'll tell you. I put my books at the foot of the stairs, washed my hands in the downstairs bathroom, then went into the kitchen.

"How was school, honey?" My mom asked as she knelt down and kissed me, her long brown hair brushing against my face. Mom always calls me honey, or sweetie, unless she's mad at me.

"Fine," I answered, getting the silverware out of the drawer. "Except for Miss Green's science class."

"Okay. What happened?"

"Nothing, really," I said. "It's just that I want to do one science project, and Miss Green wants me to do another."

"Better do as your teacher says," said my mom.

"But, mom," I protested. "Miss Green wants me to do my project on *lipstick*."

"And what is wrong with that?"

"I don't want to do my project on lipstick," I said. "That's what's wrong with it."

I heard a car pull into the driveway. Dad was home. Good — at least he'd understand.

"It's me," I heard my dad say as Lambchop started barking. Then there were footsteps coming up the walkway. They stopped. Dad must have been rubbing Waffle's stomach. "Ouch!" came a cry.

The door swung open and my dad walked in, carrying his briefcase. He had his thumb in his mouth. "Darn cat bit me. The dog's barking. What a welcome-home-party those two make."

My dad gave my mom a kiss. And I mean a K-I-S-S. I couldn't hold my breath that long — no matter how much I liked somebody.

"How was your day?" my mom asked, as she always asked.

"The usual," my dad answered, as he always answered. My dad always waited until we sat down for dinner to tell us what his day was really like.

Dad gave me a big hug. "How was school?" he asked.

"The usual," I answered.

"That's not what I heard," said my mother, giving my father the eye.

"Tell me about it," said my father in his serious voice. He didn't like anything going wrong at school.

I told him the whole story, all about human photosynthesis, and the Science Fair, and the silver trophy, and Miss Green, and her stupid lipstick project.

"I'm sorry to say this," said my father when I had finished, "but your teacher's right."

"She's what?"

"Now hear me out," began my father, which was his usual beginning when he had something to tell me that he knew I didn't want to hear. "Nine-year-old boys just don't go around making discoveries. Especially like the mystery of human photosynthesis. You're not talking about an invention, like developing a new machine. You're talking about a discovery, which is unlocking a secret of nature. Very few major discoveries have been made since the beginning of time, and the men who made them are considered the most important men in history."

"So?"

"So none of them were nine years old."

"Then I'll be the first."

"Son, listen to me." My dad took hold of both my shoulders. "Do your project on lipstick as Miss Green wants you to. Do something you know you can do."

"Hogwash!" said a voice.

We all turned to see Grandpop standing in the doorway. "Let the boy find out for himself what he can and cannot do."

"But what Allen is talking about is impossible," insisted my father.

"It's not impossible," I said. "I don't care what anybody says. I'm going to do it. I'm going to solve the mystery of human photosynthesis."

3.

Research

The next day Grandpop and I had a secret meeting under the avocado tree in the backyard. We talked in whispers even though we knew my mom and dad were asleep. They always sleep in on Saturdays.

"Do you think I can really do it, Grandpop?" I whispered, zipping up my windbreaker. It was cold and damp under the avocado tree, and it smelled like dead leaves.

Grandpop didn't say anything as he stooped to pick up an avocado that had fallen on the ground. He rubbed the fruit with both hands, then he took out his gold-plated penknife and began to cut the avocado.

"A discovery," Grandpop began in a low whisper, "is like an avocado that has been cut into many pieces, and then the pieces hidden in different places. Some pieces are very hard to find. Others are right in front of your nose, so close, in fact, that you cannot see them. It is your job, Allen, the job of any scientist, any thinker, to find the different pieces, one by one, and then put them in their proper order until, at last, you can see . . ."

"The avocado," I said, forgetting to whisper.

"Right . . . and wrong." Grandpop held up the avocado in his hand and then turned it around to show that he had cut away the back half.

I thought for a moment before I figured out what Grandpop was trying to tell me. "You don't have to find *all* the pieces to see the *whole* picture."

"Right!" Grandpop threw the avocado to the ground and slapped his knee. He put his hand on my shoulder and the wrinkles around his eyes formed a smile. "You are a smart boy, Allen Brewster."

"But how do I find the pieces, Grandpop?"

"You must use the same *tools* that all the great discoverers of the past have used."

"Are they expensive? I don't have much money."

"You do not have to buy these tools, Allen. They are free. You were born with them."

"I was? What are they?"

Grandpop led me out from underneath the avocado tree into the bright sunlight that now filled the backyard. He held out his arms and looked around as he spoke. "There are only six tools, Allen. The first five are your eyes, your ears, your nose, your mouth, and your fingers or skin."

"The five senses. Sight, hearing, smell, taste and touch. We learned that in school. What's the sixth tool, Grandpop?"

"The sixth tool is the most important but, I'm sorry to say, the least used." He pointed to his head. "It's your *brain*. Without your brain, all the pieces of information you obtain with the other five tools are useless. Without your brain, without thinking, no discovery is possible."

"Then I must learn everything I can about photosynthesis, and about plants and animals, and the difference between them. After that I can use the sixth tool, my brain, to make my discovery."

"Right! Right! Right!" Grandpop hopped from one foot to the other as he spoke. "I can see your name in the encyclopedia now. . . . Allen Brewster; the discoverer of *human photosynthesis*."

We both jumped as high as we could into the air,

letting out a yell which was so loud it woke up my parents.

I powered down my breakfast so fast that I think I actually drank half my fried egg. I wanted to get to the library right away and begin my research.

Too bad my father had other ideas.

"Let's go into the living room, son," he said. "I have something I want to show you."

"But dad, the library'll be open in fifteen minutes and I want to get started on my science project."

"That's exactly what I want to talk to you about." My dad smiled. He was sure being friendly.

For the next half hour we sat on the couch in the living room and read the encyclopedia together. We read about — you guessed it — lipstick.

"I'd like to help you," my dad said. "We'll take some photographs and blow them up. Lots of charts. And we'll come up with different colors, colors no one's ever come up with before, like . . . tomato yellow. Your mother has promised to wear a different shade every Tuesday when she goes bowling."

"That's right," said my mom, poking her head around the corner. She was smiling but I noticed her eyes didn't look very happy.

"Thanks a lot," I said, getting to my feet. I realized it would be pointless to get into another argument, plus, I didn't want to waste the time, so I just said, "I'll let you know if I need any help."

A fifteen-minute bike ride later I was at the city library. With my notebook in hand, I ran up the wide stone steps to the entrance, pulled open one of the heavy glass doors and hurried inside.

"Good morning, Mrs. Snodgrass," I said to the elderly woman who sat at the reference desk. The kids called her "The Sergeant" because she was so strict.

Mrs. Snodgrass put one finger to her lips, reminding me to whisper. "What brings you here so early, Allen Brewster?"

"I'm going to make a discovery," I whispered. "It's for my science project at school."

"My goodness," said Mrs. Snodgrass, touching her hand to her face. "That sounds difficult."

"Yes, very difficult," I agreed. And then I pointed to my head. "You have to use this up here."

After I told Mrs. Snodgrass what my project was all about, she directed me over to a special part of the library.

"The books in this section are devoted to *biology*," she explained, "which is the study of living things."

"Like plants and animals."

"Yes, Allen, except we call the study of plants, *botany*, and the study of animals, *zoology*." She smiled. "Good luck."

"Thank you, Mrs. Snodgrass."

I looked at every book I could get my hands on, especially the ones that mentioned photosynthesis in the index. I took notes as I went. I wrote so much my hand began to ache. And when I stopped writing I had to straighten out my fingers one by one.

I took a break to stretch and get a drink of water.

The library had filled up. I saw several kids from school doing research on their projects. I saw Peggy Applegate. When she saw me, she said something to her girl friends and they all looked over and started giggling. She must have told them my project was on lipstick.

I looked around for Barry Cramer. I didn't see him. Good. It must be my lucky day, I remembered saying to myself.

Or, so I thought.

When I went back to my table, there he was. He

was sitting in my chair, reading my notebook. When I approached, he just looked at me and grinned.

Then he began to read out loud, "For photosynthesis to work," he said, grinning after each word, "the following ingredients are needed: water, carbon dioxide, sunlight, and chlorophyll."

"Give me my notebook," I said.

"Not so fast. I haven't got to the good part, yet." He gave me another sickening grin.

Several kids had begun to gather around, including Peggy Applegate and her silly friends.

"Hemoglobin," Barry continued reading from my notebook, "in our blood makes it red ... chlorophyll in a plant makes it green. Could there be a *connection*?" Barry rolled his eyes around and stuck his tongue out of the side of his mouth.

Everyone laughed.

"Get out of my chair," I snarled, trying to look as mean as possible.

"Make me," said Barry, giving me his meanest look, which, I'll be the first to admit, was pretty good.

It was at this time that I noticed Mrs. Snodgrass heading over in our direction. She had obviously heard all the noise and was coming to investigate. One look at her gave me an idea.

"The least you can do is speak up," I told Barry. "If you're going to read something important, you might as well say it so everyone can hear you."

This got a laugh. Not a real big one, but just enough to make Barry mad, which was just what I wanted.

Barry stood up and began to read loudly from my notebook. "For *human photosynthesis* to be possible, the hemoglobin in our blood must somehow act as chlorophyll does in a plant. . . ."

"It's the Sergeant!" someone said, and everyone scattered.

But it was too late for Barry Cramer. Mrs. Snodgrass had him by the ear. She then proceeded to lead him out of the library. I snatched my notebook from Barry's hand as they went by.

I sat back down at my table, breathed a sigh of relief, and continued my research.

Hours went by. I don't know how many.

"Human blood," I said to myself, chewing on the end of my pen. "That had to be it. Everything pointed to it. But did human blood contain all the necessary ingredients for photosynthesis to take place?"

I wrote the following down in my notebook:

Necessary for Photosynthesis	Human Blood
1. Water	1. Blood is mostly water.
2. Carbon dioxide	2. Blood carries carbon dioxide to our lungs where it's exhaled.
3. Sunlight	3. Blood uses absorbed sunlight through our skin to make Vitamin D.
4. Chlorophyll	4. Blood contains hemoglobin which has a similar chemical structure to chlorophyll.

What did Grandpop used to say? "Close is only good in horseshoes." Just because hemoglobin was close to chlorophyll didn't mean anything. They would have to be the same. Somehow there must be a way to make them the same.

As I reached for another book, I heard my name. "Allen Brewster?"

I turned around quickly and saw the Sergeant.

"Are you still here?" said Mrs. Snodgrass. "I was

just locking up. Am I ever glad I checked one more time or you would have had to spend the night."

"I'll spend the night," I said. "I don't mind. You see, I'm right on the verge of making my discovery. I can't go, Mrs. Snodgrass. Not now — please."

"Don't be foolish, young man. Now get your things together while I turn out the lights."

"But, Mrs. Snodgrass . . ."

"I'm sorry, Allen. Your discovery will just have to wait."

4

Discovery

The next day I did not go back to the library. In fact, I did not go anyplace. I was not allowed to. It seems my parents were very upset that I had stayed so late at the library, especially when I let it slip that I had not been working on my lipstick project.

At first I was upset too, but the way things turned out, I was sure glad I stayed home that day.

I spent the morning in my room reading over my notebook. In the afternoon, when my father was asleep on the couch and my mother was in the den playing the piano, I slipped out the back door to talk to Grandpop.

Grandpop was resting in a lounge chair on the back porch, listening to some old records on his old phonograph. I motioned for him to be quiet until I had shut the back door. He turned up the volume on the phonograph a little. We both nodded, agreeing that it was safe to talk.

"Tell me more about yesterday," he said.

"Let me show you my notebook," I said.

"No. Scientists work better alone. Just tell me what you found out."

"I think I've found all the pieces to the picture but one. I'm sure if I could have stayed at the library just a little longer. . . ."

"Aren't you forgetting something, Allen?"

"What's that?"

"Remember the avocado I showed you that was really only half an avocado?"

"Yes, I remember. Then you mean I don't have to find the last piece to make my discovery?"

"Just enough pieces, arranged in the proper order, so you can almost see the whole picture. . . . Then you must use the sixth tool." He pointed to his head.

"Like the time I took my bike apart and tried to put it back together again. The pieces had to fit just a certain way, but I couldn't remember."

"So what did you do?"

"I tried every combination I could think of until I finally found the right way."

Grandpop pointed to his head.

"But I've tried, Grandpop. I've tried putting the pieces together. I just can't seem to see the picture."

"Have you tried thinking *crazy*?"

"Crazy?"

Grandpop smiled, and his eyes twinkled. "If I were to tell you," he said, "that you could whisper and someone halfway around the world in China could hear you, would you think I was crazy?"

"Sure." I laughed.

"What if I were whispering into a telephone?"

"That's different."

"Only because you see the whole picture."

"I see what you mean."

"And if I were to tell you that the sky was filled with waves that carry pictures. . . ."

"Television."

"You're catching on. Learn to think crazy, Allen. Let your mind go. Don't be afraid to think of silly things, stupid things, things so ridiculous that you burst out laughing at the mere thought of them. That's the power of the sixth tool, Allen. To think of things that no one else has ever thought of before."

"I understand."

With that Grandpop put on another record, leaned back in his lounge chair, and closed his eyes.

I opened my notebook to a clean page and wrote

the words THINK CRAZY. Directly below it, I made
the following two lists:

Plant Photosynthesis	Human Photosynthesis
1. Water	1. Water
2. Carbon Dioxide	2. Carbon Dioxide
3. Chlorophyll	3. Hemoglobin

The first list contained the necessary ingredients
which in the presence of sunlight made photosynthesis possible in plants. The second list contained
three substances found in our blood.

I ran head on into the same old problem. The
missing piece. How to make the hemoglobin in our
blood do what chlorophyll does in plants? But
Grandpop said that I didn't need to find all the
pieces. All I had to do was "think crazy."

Okay, Allen Brewster, you may begin now.

Go ahead. No one's looking.

Think.

I couldn't think.

Try.

I closed my eyes real tight.

Nothing.

All I could think about was the music from Grandpop's phonograph record. The music. That record. What was it? Something Grandpop had told me. A story. About a workman at a company. A company that gold plated records. The workman dropped a cheese sandwich into the vat of gold. Didn't tell anyone. The gold plating was better than they had ever seen before. The workman confessed. They had the workman's wife make a whole lot of cheese sandwiches. They kept adding them to the vat of gold until they had the sandwich analyzed in a laboratory, and found out that it was the sodium in the cheese that was the missing ingredient.

Think crazy. Think crazy.

The next thing I knew, I was in the kitchen opening cupboards.

"Was there something I could eat," I said to myself, "that would make the hemoglobin in my blood act as chlorophyll does in plants?"

The whole picture. Try to see the whole picture.

I started to make myself a cheese sandwich. I stopped. Wait a minute, I thought. I've had a cheese sandwich before. Lots of them. That can't be it.

"Perhaps," I said to myself, it's a combination of different things — just the right things, just the right amounts.

But what things?

Think crazy.

Anything? Just try anything?

That's too many things to try.

And then it hit me.

I ran and got my notebook. I sat down at the kitchen table and began flipping through the pages. I had written something down. All I had to do was find it.

There it was!

In my notebook, I had written the following chemical formulas:

$$\text{Chlorophyll} - C_{55}H_{72}O_5N_4Mg$$
$$\text{Hemoglobin} - C_{34}H_{32}O_4N_4Fe$$

The biggest difference between these two substances was that chlorophyll contained Mg (magnesium), whereas hemoglobin contained Fe (iron).

Think crazy.

"I will only try those things that contain magnesium," I said, hitting my fist on the kitchen table.

I tiptoed into the living room past my father who was still asleep on the couch. I selected the M volume of the encyclopedia and returned to the kitchen. I looked up the word "magnesium" and found the following list of foods had it: beans, nuts, whole grain cereal, and *liver*.

Wouldn't you know it? I can't stand liver.

I also read that salt water contained magnesium.

"Think crazy," I repeated the words.

I plugged in Mom's blender and started throwing things in, careful to write down in my notebook exactly how much of each thing.

The only beans we had were some leftover Mexican refried beans. Using the ice cream scooper, I put in one scoop. I found a can of mixed nuts in the cupboard but it was practically empty. I decided to use peanut butter instead (one scoop). We were all out of that natural cereal so I substituted Coco-Puffs (half a cup).

I found some raw liver in the refrigerator. I cut off the smallest piece I thought might work.

I was about to add some tap water to the blender when I remembered that the encyclopedia had mentioned salt water. Dad would kill me if he ever found out, but I went upstairs and took a half-cup of salt water from his aquarium, being careful not to scoop out any fish.

I turned on the blender and my concoction turned into a thick dark liquid.

I poured myself a glass.

I drank it.

That night I didn't eat any dinner. I wasn't hungry. Not one bit.

"I've done it," I told Grandpop before I went to bed. "I'll never have to eat again."

But I was wrong.

The next day when I woke up, I was starving. Beside my regular breakfast, I had an extra bowl of cereal and two extra glasses of milk.

A few days later, I repeated the experiment.

Grandpop helped me measure out each ingredient. This time I added more liver.

Again, I went to bed without eating dinner. And the next morning I still wasn't hungry. I even gave away my lunch at school.

I had done it. I was sure of it.

Wrong.

By dinner-time I was so hungry I was the first one at the table.

"Stop chewing on your hand," my mother snapped at me as she served the food.

"Sorry," I responded, not aware of what I was doing.

I had three helpings. Food never tasted so good.

But I didn't give up.

I performed my third experiment the following Sunday afternoon, after my parents had gone for a drive. They had asked Grandpop and me to go along, but we had declined — we had work to do.

"It seems the more liver I add," I told Grandpop, "the longer I can go without eating."

"You know," said Grandpop, his eyes widening, "I think you've got something there."

Mom had just gone to the store that morning, so there was plenty of liver in the refrigerator. I took out a huge, slimy piece and laid it on the counter-top. I was about to cut some off when I stopped.

"In the name of science," I shrugged, and I threw the whole piece into the blender. I added the other ingredients.

I ran the blender for an extra couple of minutes, just to make sure all the liver got dissolved.

I poured myself a glass.

Did it ever look gross. I shut my eyes. I held my nose. I took a big gulp. It tasted just like *liquid liver*. I tried to take another sip, but I just couldn't.

That night I didn't eat dinner. My stomach felt funny. I also felt real light-headed. When I opened my eyes the room would start to spin around.

My mom was worried about me. She sat on the edge of my bed and rubbed my back until I fell asleep.

I woke up in the middle of the night.

Was I thirsty! I mean, I felt like I could drink the whole Atlantic Ocean, that is, if it weren't salt water.

I made my way down the hallway, past Grand-pop's room, to the bathroom. I turned on the light, opened the medicine cabinet and took out my drinking glass. I filled it with water and drank. Water never tasted so good. I refilled my glass and drank again and again. And again.

When I was on my sixth glass, I noticed myself in the mirror.

I froze. I couldn't believe what I was looking at.

"I've done it," I said to myself, very faintly at first, then I said it louder. "I've done it! I've done it!" I began to jump around, shouting at the top of my lungs.

My mother was the first to arrive, appearing in the doorway to the bathroom. She took one look at me then put her hands over her mouth.

Dad arrived next. "What have you done to yourself?"

"He's solved the mystery," said Grandpop, as he wedged himself in between them. "That's what he's done." Grandpop was smiling from ear to ear.

I looked at myself in the mirror again. I looked perfectly normal really, except for one small change. My skin had turned bright *green*, the color of a leaf on a tree.

5.

Reaction

My folks drove me right to the hospital.

Grandpop didn't go with us. He just laughed and went back to bed, saying that what I needed was a "green thumb," not some greenhorn doctor.

At the hospital, I was examined by a tall, skinny doctor whose eyes were so close together his eyebrows touched.

"Although I've never seen anything quite like this before," he told my parents, "all tests show your son to be in excellent health. I would say you have nothing to worry about."

"Nothing to worry about?" gasped my mother, putting her arms around me. "Then why does he look like this?"

"You mean the green color? I honestly don't know."

"But . . ." said my father, "you're a doctor."

"So? We don't know everything."

"I've told you, all of you," I spoke up. "I've solved the mystery of human photosynthesis."

"He has quite an imagination, doesn't he?" said the doctor, wiggling his eyebrows as he talked.

"I'm afraid so," said my mother.

"It's his grandfather," said my father. "He's always encouraging him."

"Imagination?" I said, holding up my green arm. "What do you call this?"

"Probably nothing more than an allergic reaction to something you ate," said the doctor. "It should clear up in a few days."

"Should I keep him home from school?" my mother asked.

"No reason to do that," said the doctor. "Allergies aren't contagious."

When we got home it was just starting to get light. We live on a hill with a beautiful view of the city below. As dad pulled the car into the driveway, I could just see the sun peeking its head up over the horizon. It was such a beautiful sight I found I couldn't take my eyes off it.

My parents went into the house, but I just stood there on the lawn, watching the sun. It was as if I were seeing it for the first time.

Slivers of light streaked across the sky and then a bright yellow ball lifted its head up and shone on my face. As the sun's rays struck my body, I felt the most peculiar sensation. It was as if I were being tickled by a thousand feathers. I started to make giggling sounds and I got goose bumps on my arms.

I held up my arm and looked at it. The green color seemed almost transparent. I swear I could see my veins and the blood flowing through them.

"Honey," said my mom from the front door. "Come in and wash up for breakfast."

"In a minute." I kept my face in the sun. I felt so good at that very moment, I didn't want it to end. I could sense the grass and the other plants around me coming to life. I belonged outside with them, in the sun, not indoors.

I heard my mother raise her voice. "Come in the house this minute!"

"Okay," I answered, and I started to walk towards the house. But after a few steps, I stopped. I turned

and faced the sun again. The sun. The sun felt so good.

I vaguely remember my mother running over to me and giving me a swat on the rear end. "When I say move it . . ."

But I didn't move. I stayed right there.

I remember hearing my own voice then, trying

to explain to my mother about the sun. My voice sounded strange, like it belonged to someone else. Then there was laughter. I was laughing.

My father came into view. He took hold of one of my arms and pulled. I fell over onto the wet grass. My father threw me over his shoulder and carried me into the house.

The moment we were inside, out of the sun, I came to my senses. I still felt a little dizzy but that was about all.

"Are you all right, son?" asked my father.

"I'm fine now, thanks," I said. "It was the sun. It had some power over me."

My mom and dad looked at each other. They didn't say anything.

For breakfast, mom had made some hot cakes and sausages, smothered in maple syrup. My favorite. I even put syrup right on the sausages.

But the strangest thing happened.

I couldn't eat.

"What's wrong, honey?" asked my mom. "I thought you liked pancakes."

"I do. It's just that . . . I know you're not going to believe me, but I don't think I have to eat anymore."

"You don't have to eat?" said my mother.

"You see," I started to explain, "now that I've solved the mystery of human . . ."

"Eat your breakfast," snapped my father, looking over the top of the newspaper he was reading. "Right now."

I put a big mouthful of food into my mouth. But I couldn't chew it. I tried, but I just couldn't do it.

My father looked over his paper again. "Swallow it," he commanded when he saw my cheeks puffed out.

I shook my head no.

Before my father could say anything, I got sick. But I was able to get to the bathroom in time.

The school bus came at seven-thirty.

Somehow my body had gotten used to the sun, for I was able to go outside without becoming paralyzed. The sun still felt good. In fact, when it warmed my face, I couldn't help smiling.

I played with Waffle and Lambchop on the front lawn until I saw the bus coming, then I ran across the street and hopped on.

There are kids at our school with brown skin and kids with black skin, but I knew that a kid with green skin would just be too much.

Boy, was I right.

The moment I stepped onto the bus the place went crazy. The kids started laughing their heads off. And they wouldn't stop laughing. Barry Cramer laughed so hard he slipped off his seat onto the floor of the bus.

It was only after Ivan pulled the bus over to the side of the road and threatened to throw the next kid off who dared make a sound, that they stopped.

"What's wrong with you?" whispered Peggy Applegate from the seat right behind me.

"Nothing's wrong with me," I whispered back.

"Then why do you look like that?"

"It's part of my science project."

"I thought your project was on lipstick."

"It was, but I'm doing something else."

"You mean *human photosynthesis*?"

"That's right."

"What are you supposed to be — a plant?" Peggy began to giggle. "Let me see your outline."

"What outline?"

"The one that's due today. Or, did you forget?"

I did forget. Miss Green had wanted everyone to hand in an outline, showing what they were going to do on their projects. I was so busy making my discovery that I had forgotten all about it.

"Doesn't matter," I told Peggy over my shoulder. "When I tell Miss Green what I've done, she'll understand."

How wrong I was.

"What do you think you're doing, Allen Brewster?" shouted Miss Green the moment I walked into the classroom. She really blew her stack. "What do you mean coming to my class looking like someone on his way to a halloween party?"

"You don't understand, Miss Green."

"I do understand," she said, her lower lip curling up. "Today just happens to be the day your outline is due. Your project is on lipstick. Do you have yours with you?"

"If you'll just give me a chance to explain."

"Do you have your outline?"

"No."

"Just as I thought."

"But look at me," I said. "Can't you see . . ."

"I see a clown who has not done his homework. I will not have my classroom turned into a circus with your ridiculous pranks. Now go to the restroom this minute and wash off that green paint."

"It's not paint."

"Out!" shouted Miss Green, pointing to the door. "And don't come back until you look like a normal human being."

6.

Proof

Can you believe it? I had a project that was sure to win the silver trophy, not to mention Miss Green would probably get voted best science teacher, and what happens? She won't even listen to me.

I also had another problem. Miss Green had told me not to come back until I had washed off the green paint. Except it wasn't green paint, and I didn't know how to change myself back.

As I walked home, I decided there was only one thing for me to do. I had to figure out a way to *prove* to Miss Green what I had done. What else could I do?

"But how?" I asked myself. "How do you prove something to somebody?"

Why even my own folks didn't believe me, or the

doctor who examined me. Telling them obviously didn't work. Even seeing me didn't convince anyone. But there must be some way. People believed certain things and they didn't believe other things. Why? What made the difference?

It was a long walk home, but I didn't mind. I had to think.

I stopped at the park in the center of town and sat on a bench by the lake so I could watch the ducks. I put my lunchpail on my knees and opened it. Mom had packed me a big lunch because I hadn't eaten any breakfast.

As expected, I still wasn't hungry. I had no appetite at all. I didn't have to eat anymore. All I needed was sunlight and water. I was making my own food internally, just as a plant does. I had become a *human plant*.

I suddenly became very thirsty.

I hurried over to the drinking fountain and drank for about five minutes. When I had finished, I noticed that three people had lined up behind me. They seemed startled when they saw my green face.

"Just paint," I told them.

They all looked relieved.

How funny, I thought. They believed something that wasn't true without questioning it. But if I had told them the truth, they wouldn't have believed me no matter what I had said.

"Hi, I'm a plant. Watch me eat sunlight."

Now, let me ask you, who was going to believe that? I had to figure out a way to prove it. That's all there was to it.

I continued walking home, thinking hard. I passed shops and restaurants and service stations. I passed the City Hall, and the Plaza Hotel, and the Daily *Courier* newspaper building.

The newspaper.

Something had happened a few days ago. It was at breakfast. Mom and dad were having an argument about something. I don't remember what.

"How do you know that?" my mom had said.

"It says so right here in the newspaper," my father had answered.

That was it!

If I could somehow get my story in the newspaper, that would be all the proof I'd need. Miss Green would believe me and so would my parents and so would everybody.

I tucked in my shirt, pushed open the heavy glass doors with both hands, and walked into the newspaper building.

"You're a what?"

"I'm a plant."

"A what?"

"P-L-A-N-T." I spelled it out for the bald-headed man who wore Coke bottle glasses, and who sat behind a desk that was so piled up with papers I could barely see him. The sign on his office door had said FEATURES EDITOR.

"I know it's hard to believe," I continued, "but please hear me out."

My dad's expression worked because the man kept quiet and let me talk. Halfway through my story he stopped me. He took out a small tape recorder from his desk and had me start over.

When I had finished, the editor pressed a button and spoke into a small plastic box on his desk. "Miss Padilla," he said, "get me a photographer, and hurry." He looked at me over the tops of the piles of papers on his desk. "Do I have a beauty for tomorrow's feature."

"The editor believed me," I told Grandpop when I got home. "My story will be in tomorrow morning's newspaper. Everyone will believe me now."

Grandpop didn't seem very excited.

"Don't worry about other people," he told me. "It's not important what they think."

"You don't have Miss Green for fourth grade science," I told him.

The next morning I put on my robe and went out to the driveway to wait for the newspaper. It's supposed to be delivered at six o'clock. It was right on time.

I opened up the paper and sure enough there I was, in living color, right on the front page of Section III. It wasn't a bad picture either. I was smiling, my hands high in the air.

I put the newspaper on the kitchen table in dad's

place so he wouldn't miss it. Everything was set. All I had to do was wait.

"Would you look at this?" said my father as he sat down at the table, picking up the *wrong* section of the newspaper. "The President is coming to our city next week."

"Do you mean the President of the United States?" asked my mother.

"The one and only. Says so right here."

"What on earth for?"

"Says here he's going to be talking with members of an organization called *SWS, Stop World Starvation*. You know, the group the Applegates wanted us to join."

I wanted to scream.

There was my face right there in plain sight, right in front of my father, and he didn't see it. All he could talk about was the President and that group Peggy Applegate's parents belonged to.

Be patient, I told myself. He'll see it. Give him time.

My dad continued reading about the President.

"Allen," my mother asked me. "Do you feel like eating breakfast? I don't want you getting sick again."

"Just a glass of water, mom."

And then my father saw it.

I could tell because the scrambled eggs he had just put into his mouth came tumbling out onto his plate.

He didn't say anything for the longest time, then he just looked at me and said, "Tell me it isn't true, Allen."

"It is, dad. You can read it right there in the newspaper."

My father picked up the paper and read the head-line aloud: "Human Plant. Eats only Sunlight. The Amazing True Story of Allen Brewster." He handed

the newspaper to my mother. "What are the neighbors going to say? And the guys at the office?"

"Oh, Allen," said my mom when she saw the paper. "What have you done?"

"I've proved it. That's what I've done. I've got it in the newspaper. Now you believe me, don't you?"

"Listen to me, Allen," said my father, rubbing the back of his neck. "And, listen good. Every week this newspaper features some sensational story. Last week it was some minister getting ready to rise to heaven. The poor man had sold his house and everything. They do it to sell newspapers. It doesn't prove a thing."

"It doesn't?"

"In fact, it makes it worse."

"You mean, Miss Green won't believe me either?"

"Nobody in their right mind will believe you. And furthermore, I'm sick and tired of hearing about your discovery. I'm sick and tired of you not eating your meals. You're a nine-year-old boy like all other nine-year-old boys. You are not a plant. The discussion is closed. Do I make myself clear?"

"Yes," I said. "Very clear."

7.

Problems

I didn't know what to do.

I couldn't go to school because I was still green. I couldn't go downstairs to breakfast because I couldn't eat. So, I did the only thing I could do — I stayed in bed.

And, I don't mean for just a few hours. I stayed in bed for a whole week.

Mom thought I was just sick, so she'd bring me my meals on a tray, which I would in turn give to Waffle and Lambchop as soon as she left the room.

Peggy Applegate, who lives two houses away, brought me my homework so I didn't fall behind in my studies.

I had moved my bed over next to the window so that I would get plenty of sunlight.

I had it made — that is, until the storm.

It rained for four days and four nights. On the morning of the fifth day I woke up to find that I was so weak I couldn't move. I was totally without energy. Something was terribly wrong and I knew exactly what it was. I needed sunlight. I was going to die without it.

"I can see you're getting better," said my mother, walking into the room with a bowl of chicken soup.

"Why's that, mom?" I asked, barely able to speak.

"You don't look as green as you did yesterday."

"I don't?"

"The doctor said it would go away. See, you're a boy, after all, not a plant."

Wrong, I thought to myself. I was obviously an outdoor plant, not an indoor plant.

"Mom," I struggled to speak. "What's the weatherman say?"

"More rain. Could last another week."

Oh, great, I thought. I'll end up like that plant we had in the hallway. It turned yellow and then got droopy and died. I didn't want to die. I wasn't even a teenager yet.

But what could I do? I couldn't go to the grocery

store and buy a quart of sunlight like you could milk.

And then I thought of something — it was a long shot, but what did I have to lose?

"Would you bring my desk lamp over here?" I asked my mom.

"Would you like a book, too?"

"No. Yes." I didn't have the energy to explain. I felt myself getting real weak now.

My mother brought over the lamp and plugged it in. "Is this book all right, dear?"

"Turn it on," I whispered.

"What was that, honey?"

I was too weak to repeat what I had said. I felt my eyes close and then everything went black.

I don't know how long I was out, but when I awoke there was a bright light shining in my face. I felt better. A lot better. The desk lamp had saved my life.

There was a knock on the door.

"Allen, okay to come in?"

"Sure, Grandpop," I said, sitting up in bed.

Grandpop came in carrying the portable television set from his room. "Thought you might like to watch the tube with me."

"What's on? A monster movie?" Grandpop says he doesn't get scared if I watch them with him.

"Something about a giant cucumber that terrorizes a town."

"Great."

Grandpop put the TV on my desk. He started to bend over and plug it in.

"I got it," I said, jumping out of bed. I climbed under my desk and put the plug into the outlet.

"You seem better," he said. "Your green color's coming back. But I don't like those green dots all over your face." Grandpop put his face real close to mine.

"What green dots? Do you mean mites?"

"No," said Grandpop. "These look more like *aphids*. My peach tree's got them too."

"I don't want any bugs on me, Grandpop." I was real scared. I started brushing them off my face with my hands. And then I saw them all over my arms, and I started brushing my arms too. "Help me, Grandpop. Help me."

"Now, just hold your horses. I'll go get the sprayer."

When Grandpop returned with the sprayer, he had me stand in the shower.

"Now, keep your eyes shut real tight," he told me, "and don't breathe."

"Hurry, Grandpop. I can feel them crawling all over me."

Grandpop sprayed me real well. I showered up right afterwards. The aphids were gone — good riddance.

"How come no one but you believes I'm a plant?" I asked Grandpop as we sat down to watch the movie.

"That's easy to explain," he said, turning on the television. Grandpop had an answer for everything. "Remember the story I told you about the cheese sandwich?"

"And the vat of gold?"

"Yes. Now, if the worker had walked up to his boss one day and told him to add a cheese sandwich to the gold, what do you think his boss would have said?"

"He would have said he was crazy."

"Why?"

"Because he didn't understand."

"Right."

"So how do we make people understand, Grandpop?"

"That's the secret, Allen. You don't make them understand."

"What?"

"You tell them."

"I don't understand."

Grandpop went over to my bookcase and returned with one of my encyclopedia volumes. "You believe what's in here, don't you?"

"Yes."

"Without question. Without proof?"

"Yes."

"Why?"

"Because it wouldn't be in there if it weren't the truth."

"Why?"

"Because it's the encyclopedia."

"And an encyclopedia is respected for telling the truth."

"So we believe it."

"That's right, Allen."

"And the person who wrote about me in the newspaper wasn't respected for telling the truth, so no one believed him, even though what he wrote was the truth."

"Right again, Allen."

"So all I need to do is find someone who everyone respects, and have that person say that I'm a plant. Then everyone will believe me."

"Right a third time," said Grandpop, swinging his arm in the air.

"But where am I going to find such a person?"

Grandpop looked sad. "I don't know."

We both sat there in silence for a moment, then we turned to the television and there on the news was the President of the United States. He was giving a speech on the steps of the City Hall building in town.

Grandpop and I slowly turned our heads and looked at each other.

8.

The President

How do you go about meeting the President of the United States?

Do you just call him up on the telephone?

"Hi, I'm Allen Brewster. I'm nine years old and I was wondering if you're busy this afternoon, because if you're not, I would like to talk with you. What about? Oh, well, you see, I want you to tell everyone that I'm a plant. . . ."

It would never work. He'd think I was some kind of a nut. I couldn't tell the President why I wanted to see him until I was with him. But why would the President want to see me?

The answer to my question came the next day

when I saw the morning newspaper. There was a photograph of the President on the front page. He was standing underneath a large banner that had the letters *SWS* printed on it, and he was shaking hands with Peggy Applegate's father, Mr. Applegate.

I remembered my father mentioning an organization called *SWS* that day my picture appeared in the paper, so I read the whole article and found out that Mr. Applegate was head of the local chapter of *SWS*. *SWS* stood for an organization called *S*top *W*orld *S*tarvation. They send food to kids living in poor countries, kids that don't have enough to eat. I read that the President had promised to help *SWS* in every way he could, although he never mentioned exactly what he was going to do.

Well, I knew what to do. With my discovery, no one would ever have to go hungry again. People could simply turn themselves into plants.

I had a good reason to see the President. Now, he had a good reason to see me. But, would he want to see a nine-year-old kid? I decided to write him a letter. That way he wouldn't know how old I was, especially if I spelled all the words right.

After several attempts, this is the letter I came up with:

Dear Mr. President:

I read about you in an article
in our local newspaper. It said you
are interested in ending world
starvation. Well, I have made a
discovery that will enable you to
do this. If you are interested,
please let me know and I will tell
you what it is.
Thank you very much.
Sincerely,

Allen Brewster

Allen Brewster
Researcher

I didn't feel it was wrong to call myself a researcher — not after all I'd been through.

The newspaper had said that the President was
staying at the Plaza Hotel in town, so when I heard
my mom leave to go grocery shopping, I got dressed,
got on my bicycle, and rode over there. I was afraid
if my mom saw me, she'd think I was well enough
to go back to school. But I couldn't — not until I had
proof for Miss Green.

I gave my letter to the desk clerk at the Plaza Hotel who promised to give it to the President.

There was nothing to do then but wait.

It had rained earlier that morning but by now it was just kind of overcast.

As I stood on the back porch, I found that I could not take my eyes off a mud puddle in Grandpop's garden. As if attracted by a giant magnet, I found myself walking toward the puddle, taking off my shoes and socks as I went.

I smiled as I put one foot into the dark water. I felt the cold, slippery mud ooze between my toes. I put my other foot in. I can't describe the feeling. It was as if I somehow belonged there in Grandpop's garden, like I never wanted to leave.

I looked up and saw Grandpop staring at me.

"I'm sorry, Grandpop," I said. "I'll get out of your garden right away."

"Don't be ridiculous," replied Grandpop before I could move. "I've been saving a place for you."

"You know," I said, smiling again as I dug my toes deeper into the mud. "Plants don't have such a bad life. They're outside. Plenty of fresh air. No chores to do."

"They keep to themselves," added Grandpop.

"Don't bother anybody. Wish I could say the same for people."

"It's just too bad they can't read," I said. "I would sure miss my encyclopedias."

Just then my father appeared at the back door. He was home early from work.

"What on earth are you doing?" he yelled at me.

"Nothing," I answered, wondering what he meant.

"Get out of that mud this minute, wash up and come inside. There's someone here to see you."

Someone to see me? I wondered if it could be the President.

Grandpop sprayed my feet with the hose then gave me an old t-shirt to dry off with. As I was drying my feet, I felt some bumps on the bottom of my toes. I twisted my foot around and examined it. Just below the surface of the skin were some dark spots. They seemed to be pushing their way toward the surface.

"Grandpop!" I called out. "Come look at these."

Grandpop examined the bottom of my toes.

"Those aren't what I think they are, are they?"

"They sure are." Grandpop was smiling. "You're sprouting roots, boy."

"What if I had stayed in the mud a little longer?

Would they have taken hold? Could I have gotten away? Would I have to spend the rest of my life in the garden?"

Grandpop didn't answer me. He just began to chuckle.

"Grandpop!" I put on my shoes and socks as fast as I could and went into the house.

There were three people waiting for me in the living room. The President of the United States was not one of them. There was my mom and dad and a tall, overweight man, smoking a cigarette, who was introduced to me as Dr. Wedemeyer.

"I'm a psychiatrist," said the man, smoke coming out of his nose and mouth as he talked. "Do you know what a psychiatrist is, Allen?"

"You're a shrink."

"Allen," said my mother.

"I apologize."

Dr. Wedemeyer smiled, keeping his lips tight so as to not show his teeth. "Your parents asked me to talk with you because they are worried about you. They say you are not eating. They say you give your food to the dog and cat. Is that true?"

"Yes." All this time I thought I had them fooled. I guess my folks are pretty smart after all.

"Why don't you eat your meals?" asked Dr. Wedemeyer.

"If I tell you, you won't believe me. Nobody believes me, except Grandpop."

"Try me," said the psychiatrist as he blew smoke out of the corner of his mouth.

"Okay," I said. "I'm a plant."

"I believe you."

"You do?"

"Yes, Allen. I believe that you think you are a plant." The man snuffed his cigarette out in the ashtray. "What kind of plant are you?"

"I don't know. I never thought about it before."

"Plants have roots, Allen. Do you have roots?"

"Yes. Baby ones."

"Show them to me."

I took off my shoes and socks and showed Dr. Wedemeyer the dark spots on the bottom of my toes. I also showed my mom and dad. Mom started to cry.

Dr. Wedemeyer wrote something down in a small notebook.

"Your parents tell me that you love banana splits, Allen. Is that right?"

"They're my favorite," I said. "I mean, they used to be before I became a plant."

"I have one in the kitchen right now. Would you like it, Allen?"

"Thank you, but I'd just get sick. And anyway, I wouldn't be able to taste it."

"Why's that?"

"I don't have any taste buds anymore." I stuck out my tongue, and my mom started to cry again.

Dr. Wedemeyer touched my tongue. "He's right," he told my parents. "It's as smooth as a whistle."

"The way things are going," I said, "I wouldn't be surprised if I sprouted leaves next spring and maybe some new limbs."

Dr. Wedemeyer continued writing in his notebook. I noticed his lips moving. He looked up at me and cocked his head to the side. "Why are you standing like that, Allen?"

"Like what?" And then I noticed that I was tilted in the direction of the table lamp. I was a little embarrassed. "I'm sorry. I didn't realize. But plants do grow in the direction of the light, you know."

Dr. Wedemeyer jotted down more notes.

As I stood there watching him, I felt a sigh of relief. At last, I had been able to convince someone. I didn't need the President after all.

The psychiatrist put away his notebook and lit up another cigarette. That was his second in less than fifteen minutes.

"You have a *psychosomatic* illness," he said, smiling again, his lips tight. He leaned back on the couch and crossed his legs.

"What does psychosomatic mean?" I asked.

"It means, Allen, that it's all in your mind. You believe you're a plant. You believe it so much that you begin to act like a plant. That explains your skin color, your not eating, your roots, lack of taste buds, everything. You're a plant because you *think* you're a plant. It's all in your mind."

"I don't *think* I'm a plant," I insisted. "I *know* I'm a plant."

"Stop it," said my father, coming over to me. "You heard what Dr. Wedemeyer said. What does it take to convince you?"

"Me? What does it take to convince you?"

"Nothing will ever convince me. I don't care if you got the President of the United States to say that you're a plant, I still wouldn't believe it. You're my son. And my son is not a plant."

The doorbell rang. It was a man with a telegram.

"It's for you, Allen," said my mother with a funny look on her face as she handed me the telegram. "It's from the President of the United States."

9.
Top Secret

Things happened so quickly after that, that it's hard for me to remember everything.

The telegram said that a car would pick me up at three that afternoon. I explained all about my letter to my folks. They didn't say much. They were stunned.

At ten minutes after three, a brown car arrived with two men in it. Both men were tall and had dark hair. They both wore suits. They both had on sunglasses.

They drove me to the Plaza Hotel. We rode the elevator together to the penthouse. No one said a word.

Inside the penthouse, I was met by a white-haired

man who looked very disappointed. "Why you're just a boy," he said. "And a green boy at that."

Whoever this man was, he was *not* the President of the United States.

"I'm sorry, sir," I said. "But I was afraid that if the President knew my age, he wouldn't want to see me."

The white-haired man thought for a moment, and I noticed several rows of wrinkles appear on his forehead.

"You're right," he nodded. "He wouldn't have."

"I didn't lie, sir. If the President would've asked me, I would've told him how old I was. It was just that . . ."

The man waved his hand, indicating that he didn't want to discuss the matter any further. "I'm impressed with your cleverness."

I smiled. So was I.

"May I see the President, now?" I asked.

"He's not here."

"What?"

"The President had to return to Washington. He has a country to run, you know. But, don't worry. I'm one of the President's chief advisors. Name's Kirby, by the way."

We shook hands and Mr. Kirby led me into the

penthouse living room, which had a blue rug, white furniture, and red drapes. The view was breathtaking.

"The President," continued Mr. Kirby, "has given me strict orders to treat you with the utmost respect, so that's exactly what I am going to do — even if you are only a boy."

"I know about strict orders." I laughed. Mr. Kirby didn't.

"In your letter," said Mr. Kirby, relaxing on one of the white couches, "you mentioned something about a discovery that would end world starvation. Was that the truth, or were you just being clever again?"

"It was the honest truth, sir. I swear it."

Mr. Kirby gave me a long look, and the wrinkles on his forehead appeared again. "I'm curious how a boy your age would approach the problem." He motioned towards an overstuffed easy chair. "Have a seat and tell me about it."

I talked with the President's advisor for a whole hour. I told him all about my discovery, and about Miss Green and the silver trophy. And about my parents and Dr. Wedemeyer, and the fact that nobody believed me, except for Grandpop.

"I don't expect you to believe me either, sir, not

without proof. But I think I've figured out a way to prove it."

"How's that?" Mr. Kirby looked at me without blinking.

"You can watch me," I told him. "For a week, a month, for however long it takes. I won't eat anything. Nothing at all, except water and sunlight. Have a doctor examine me everyday. You'll see I stay healthy without eating. And if it works for me, then it will work for all the starving people in the world. What do you think?"

Mr. Kirby sat motionless for a moment, then he sprang off the couch and went into another room where I saw him make a phone call, although I couldn't hear what he said.

When he came back into the room, he looked very serious. "The President says it's a go."

"All right!"

At first, my dad said no to the whole deal, but after he received a personal phone call from the President, he changed his mind.

The next ten days went by really fast.

I stayed right there at the hotel with Mr. Kirby. We went swimming everyday and had long talks and watched TV together in the evenings. The President's advisor liked monster movies, just like Grandpop.

Just before I went to bed every night, I was examined by a team of doctors. It was really fun. They would do all kinds of tests, muttering to themselves things like "amazing" or "I can't believe it."

They also asked me lots of questions about my discovery, like what kind of peanut butter did I use? Was it creamy style or crunchy? What kind of fish did my dad have in his salt-water aquarium? You should have seen their faces when I told them that one of the ingredients I used was liver.

"How could you drink it?" one of the doctors asked, his face all twisted out of shape.

"It was rough," I told him.

The doctors told me that they had their computers working twenty-four hours a day, trying different combinations of my ingredients, hoping to duplicate my experiment. The whole thing reminded me of Grandpop's story about the cheese sandwich and the vat of gold.

At the end of ten days, during which time I had zero to eat, except water — I declined any fertilizer — the President's advisor called off the test.

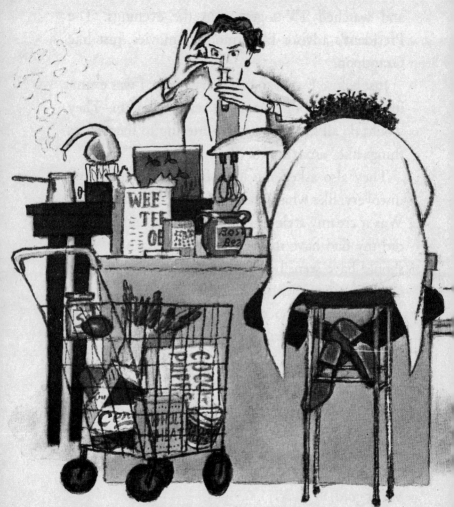

He didn't look very happy when we met together
to talk, so I asked him, "What's wrong? I proved it,
didn't I?"

Mr. Kirby didn't answer me right away. Instead,

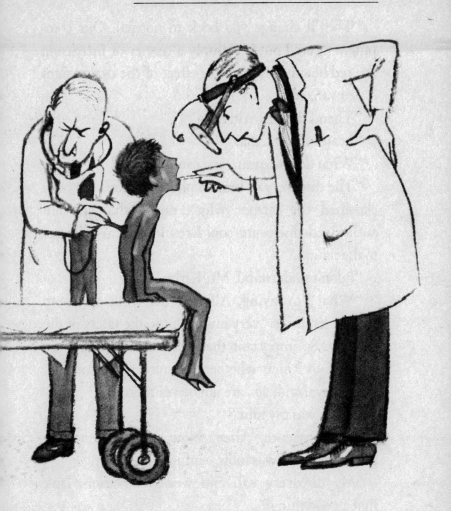

he handed me two small white pills and a glass of water. "Take one of these, Allen," he said. "And in the morning, take the second one if you have to."

"What are the pills for?"

"They'll change you back to normal. Our computers figured out it's simply a matter of increasing the red blood cells until the effect of the magnesium is neutralized."

"Then I did prove it, didn't I?"

"I can't tell you that."

"What do you mean, you can't tell me?"

"The discovery of human photosynthesis has been classified TOP SECRET, which means that any unauthorized disclosure could result in grave danger to the nation."

"I don't understand, Mr. Kirby."

"What I'm saying, Allen, is that your discovery is considered very, very important to the safety of the country. So important that only certain people are allowed to know whether it really works or not. And, I'm afraid, *you* are not one of them."

"But it was my idea."

"Not anymore, Allen. Now it belongs to the government." I was more confused than ever.

"My discovery will end world starvation. Isn't that a good thing?"

"Yes, it is. But there are many bad things about your discovery."

"Like what?" How could a discovery be bad? I wondered.

"For one thing," answered Mr. Kirby, "it would bring on the collapse of the entire economy — businesses would go broke and millions of people would lose their jobs."

"Why?"

"Because if people don't have to eat, then there would be no need for food. And did you know, Allen, that the food industry is the largest industry in the country?"

"No, I didn't."

"Your discovery would put all the farmers out of work, and all the cattlemen, and the fishermen, and all the people who process food, and package it, and transport it to market. Not to mention all the supermarkets, and restaurants, and hamburger stands. There would be no need for bread, or milk, or fruits, or vegetables, or lunch pails, or thermos bottles, or even toothpicks."

"Toothpicks?"

"If people don't eat, then they won't get food stuck in there teeth, now will they?"

"I didn't realize," I said. "But couldn't all these people find something else to do?"

"That's the second thing wrong with your discovery," said the President's advisor. "One of the main reasons people work is because they have to eat.

With your discovery, people would stop working. And if no one works, then how is the government going to stay in business? The government needs to tax people who work, that's how it gets its money. But if no one works . . . ?"

"Couldn't the government earn its money the way other people do?"

"Don't be ridiculous," Mr. Kirby laughed. "What would you have us do, sell vacuum cleaners?"

"Sure, if that will keep people from starving."

Mr. Kirby looked at me as if he had just been hit in the head by a spit-wad. "I'm sorry, Allen, but my orders come from the President himself. Your discovery is to be considered TOP SECRET. You must promise that you will never tell anyone how you did it."

"But what about my parents? And Miss Green?"

"No one. Do I have your promise?"

I looked at the floor. "Yes," I said. "I promise."

10.
The Science Fair

As it turned out, I was going to be entering a project in the Science Fair after all.

You see, the President must have felt sorry for me because he sent me a gift. Fully assembled, it stood six feet high and just as wide. It consisted of four panels of plywood hinged together, lots of photographs, charts, diagrams, a complete notebook of over a hundred pages typed, and several samples. It was a science project on LIPSTICK.

Sure, the project looked good. In fact, it would probably win an award. Sure, I was no longer green, which meant I could go back to school. Sure, my turning in a project as nice as this would mean that I would not have to take science over next year with Miss Green. Sure, I should have been happy. But I wasn't. And the reason was simple: the project wasn't mine.

I had done something really great — the discovery of human photosynthesis. It was something that no one else had ever done before, and yet I couldn't tell anybody. The President had made me promise.

My parents were happy to see me normal again and eating, but most importantly they were happy not to hear anything more about my discovery. Mr. Kirby had told them that my condition had been all in the mind, which made my father happy because he had been saying that all along.

Only Grandpop knew that something was wrong.

"What happened?" he asked as he led me by the hand out to the back porch.

"I can't tell you, Grandpop."

"You don't have to tell me," he said, kicking his foot in the air. "I can figure it out. They don't have the imagination to see how things could be different, so they try to pretend your idea doesn't exist. They hope it'll go away. But it won't. No, sir, Allen Brewster, it won't."

I didn't say anything. But I was sure glad that Grandpop believed me, even though Miss Green and my parents would never know the truth.

"Never know the truth." I found myself repeating the words.

Why hadn't I thought of it before? It was the perfect way to convince Miss Green, to prove to her once and for all, and yet, at the same time, keep my promise to the President.

It wasn't going to be easy. In fact, there was a big chance it wouldn't work. But I was sure going to give it a try. I raced upstairs to my room.

I had work to do.

The day of the Science Fair arrived.

The Science Fair is one of the biggest things to happen in our town every year. Grammar schools and high schools from all over the county are represented. It's an all-day affair, held on the grounds of the State College. The judging of the projects, which are on display in the gym, is done in the morning. Then, in the afternoon, it's over to the auditorium where the awards are given out. After that, there's a big picnic on the football field. It's potluck, which means that everybody is supposed to bring something. Mom was bringing a liver casserole.

I got up early and rode my bike over to the fair. The night before my dad and I had set up my project in the gym like all the other kids. I wanted to check over my project one more time before the judging started. If my plan was going to work, everything had to be perfect.

As I walked in the entrance to the gym, I ran head-on into Miss Green. I might as well have run into a truck.

"I just saw your project," said Miss Green as she picked me up off the floor and dusted me off. "I thought for sure I was going to have to flunk you, Allen Brewster, but with a project as nice as that, I just can't."

"Thank you," I said.

The judging took place at ten o'clock. Each student was required to stand by his project to answer questions. Peggy Applegate was on one side of me with her ant farm. Barry Cramer was on the other side with a project on motorcycle compression ratios, which his father probably did for him.

It wasn't until the judges were talking to Peggy that I noticed my lipstick samples were missing. I looked over at Barry. His pockets were bulging. "Something bothering you?" he said to me with that sickening grin of his.

I hadn't counted on this. That idiot Barry Cramer was going to mess up my plan.

As I was thinking of what to do, the judges gathered around my project.

"Excellent," said the first judge, adjusting his glasses as he looked at my photographs and charts.

"Fine job," said the second judge, who was wearing white gloves, as she thumbed through my notebook.

"Do you have any samples?" asked the third judge, a tall man with a pointed beard.

"Yes, sir," I answered.

"Where are they? I don't see them."

"I gave them to my assistant to polish." I looked over at Barry Cramer, and so did the judges. "You're finished polishing them, aren't you, Barry?"

"What are you talking about?" said Barry, nervously.

I pointed at his bulging pockets. "I'm talking about those lipsticks in your pockets."

Barry realized he was caught and handed them over.

"He's a little forgetful," I told the judges, "but he does good work." I gave the lipsticks to the judges to examine.

A half hour later, the judges came back and pinned a blue ribbon on my project. I had won best science project for a fourth-grader.

I can't tell you how bad that made me feel. It was so dishonest. Some of those kids had really worked hard. I hadn't done a thing. The blue ribbon didn't belong to me. I realized right then and there that I couldn't accept it.

As I was about to say something to one of the judges, Miss Green came up to me and planted a big slobbery kiss on my cheek.

"Congratulations, Allen," she said.

"Thanks." I wiped my cheek with my shirt sleeve. I had never seen Miss Green like this before. She was almost human.

"I'm so proud of you." She just stood there, staring at me.

"It was nothing, really."

And then I decided it was time. Motioning towards my lipstick samples, I asked her, "Would you like one of these, Miss Green?"

"For me?" She pointed her thumb toward her chest.

"Yes. But I would like to ask you a favor."

"Anything, Allen."

"Would you put it on?"

Miss Green hesitated. "I don't normally wear lipstick. . . ."

"Please. It would mean a whole lot to me."

"Okay, for you, I'll do it." Miss Green examined the samples, reading the different names. "I think I'll try Tomato Yellow."

"Good choice," I said, smiling.

I watched as Miss Green smeared on the lipstick. Her lips were large, especially the lower one that curled up, and she used a lot. Then, just as my mom does, Miss Green ran her tongue all around her lips, licking them.

11.

The Awards

Everything was going according to plan.

At one o'clock it was time for the public presentation of awards and we all crowded into the auditorium.

A few minutes earlier I had gone out to the parking lot and had found Miss Green's car. I wrote down her license number on a piece of paper. All part of the plan.

Inside the auditorium, I was shocked to see so many people. Nearly every seat was taken. On the stage there was a row of chairs with distinguished-looking people sitting in them, and off to the right, a podium with a microphone. Below the stage were the awards spread out on three long tables. Right in the middle of the center table was the *sliver trophy*. It was all polished and shined up, and really looked beautiful.

I waved to my mom and dad and Grandpop, who arrived just as the first speaker stepped to the podium. I was glad they were late, which meant they would be sitting in the back of the auditorium and wouldn't be able to see what was going to happen.

I didn't sit with them because all students were supposed to sit with their science teacher in pre-assigned rows of seats. I made sure I was sitting right next to Miss Green.

It was all part of the plan.

The speeches were long and boring. The way some of those people talked, you'd have thought they had done all the work.

I looked at my watch. I looked at Miss Green. I checked my pockets. In one pocket I had a small mirror which I had brought from home. In my other pocket I had a cookie. All part of the plan.

A tall man with orange hair and wearing a checkered suit stepped behind the podium and began reading off the names of the winners, who in turn came forward and picked up their awards. There was a lot of noise and applause after each name was called.

He had started with the grade school awards first, then he would go on to the high school awards, and then last, the grand prize — the silver trophy.

I looked at my watch again. I looked at Miss Green, studying her face. I went over the plan one more time in my mind.

And then it was time.

"Miss Green." I tugged on her sleeve.

"What is it, Allen?" said Miss Green, obviously annoyed that I was interfering with her enjoyment of the award ceremonies.

"Is this the license number of your car?" I handed Miss Green the slip of paper.

"Why, yes," she said, examining the numbers. "I believe it is. What of it?"

"You left your lights on. I'm sorry I forgot to tell you before."

"I did what?"

"Your lights. I noticed them when I walked over here from the gym. I came right through the parking lot."

"Are you sure it was my car, Allen?"

"Positive, Miss Green. That's why I took down the license number. Just to be sure."

Miss Green made her way to the aisle, then went out the side exit to the parking lot. I followed. I had to get Miss Green away from everybody, and I didn't have much time.

Outside, I ran up to Miss Green, taking her by the arm. "You better hurry, Miss Green. Before the battery goes dead."

"You're right, Allen," she said, taking longer strides across the parking lot. "I hope we're in time."

When we got to the car, Miss Green noticed immediately that her lights were *not* on.

"I'm sorry, Miss Green," I said. "I've pulled a trick on you."

"You've what?" Miss Green's eyes narrowed. "You better have a good explanation for this."

"I have," I answered. "But I want you to promise to hear me out. It will only take five minutes."

Miss Green looked back across the parking lot to the auditorium. "But you'll miss your award, Allen."

"This is more important to me," I told her.

"It is?"

"Yes."

Miss Green studied my face. "Go ahead, Allen."

I proceeded to tell her the whole story. Right from the beginning. Everything. Even about the lipstick project that wasn't mine, and about my promise to the President.

"I'm not breaking my promise to the President,"

I said, "because I'm not going to tell you *how* it works, I'm only going to convince you that it does work. I don't expect you to believe me without proof, but I have the proof. Believe me, I have all the proof you'll ever need. All I want is for you to believe me, Miss Green."

Miss Green scratched the underside of her chin, her eyes thin slits as she studied me.

"Let's see the proof, Allen."

I reached into my pocket and took out the mirror and held it up to Miss Green's face so she could see herself.

"You're the proof, Miss Green. I've turned you into a plant."

12.
The Silver Trophy

"You've done *what*?" Miss Green snatched the mirror out of my hand and looked at herself. She had turned bright green. She let out a bloodcurdling scream. "Look what you've *done* to me!" She pulled at her cheeks, rubbed her forehead.

"Don't worry," I said, holding out a white pill in my hand. "I have the antidote so you can change yourself back. It only takes five minutes. The President's advisor gave me two pills, but I only needed one."

Miss Green was still studying herself in the mirror. "How? How did you do it?"

"The lipstick I gave you. I made it very concentrated, which made it very fast-acting. After you put on the lipstick, you licked your lips. That's all it took."

"What was in the lipstick, Allen?"

"I can't tell you that. It's a secret. TOP SECRET."

"Are you sure I'm a plant, Allen?" Miss Green couldn't take her eyes off the mirror. "Are you absolutely sure?"

I reached into my pocket and took out the cookie. "Try and eat this. You'll see."

Miss Green tried to take a bite of the cookie but couldn't. "I can't do it," she said. "I felt as if I was going to get sick."

"Feel your tongue," I said.

"It's so smooth," said Miss Green.

"Your taste buds are disappearing. You don't need them anymore. Also, be careful not to stand in mud or sand for too long without moving. Your roots might take hold."

"Roots?" Miss Green looked frightened.

"It's not as easy as you think being a plant. You've got to get plenty of sun, and drink lots of water, and watch out for aphids. But don't worry; if you take this pill you'll be back to normal in no time."

I handed Miss Green the pill.

She held it in her hand for a long time, just looking at it. "Don't you realize, Allen," she said, "how important this discovery is? I've waited twenty years to find someone like you in my class. I'm not going to keep quiet about this. I'm going to tell everyone I know. I'm going to scream it from the rooftops!"

"You're wasting your time," I laughed. "No one will believe you. And anyway, the President's advisor said that it would be bad for the country."

"Phooey!" said Miss Green. "The truth must not be silenced. You shouldn't have told them in the first place."

"What other choice did I have? No one else would listen to me."

"Simply write it down, Allen. Let the future be your judge. Not the present."

With that Miss Green threw the pill with all her might, sending it half-way across the parking lot.

"I'm going back over to the auditorium," she told me. "I'm going to grab the microphone and announce it to the world. Do you have anymore lipsticks, so we can prove it to the dimwits who don't believe us?"

"Yes," I said. "I didn't know which color you'd pick so I made up a whole bunch. They're with my project."

"Good. Go get them."

I hesitated. "Miss Green, I have a question."

"Shoot."

"Do you think my discovery will win the silver trophy?"

Miss Green smiled, something I'd never seen her do before. "You bet your bottom dollar. Now hurry!"

I took off, running towards the entrance to the gym to get the lipsticks.

Miss Green took off, running across the parking lot to the auditorium.

I looked back over my shoulder just in time to see two men jump out of a brown car and grab Miss Green. They shoved her into the back seat of the car and drove off.

It happened so fast there was nothing I could do.

Epilogue

My flashlight is so dim now that I can barely see to write these last few words. . . .

It was announced at school that Miss Green had been transferred to another district, although no one seemed to know exactly where.

Grandpop thinks something bad has happened to her. He says she's probably been planted somewhere.

I'm not sure.

What do you think?

Speaking of you, now that you've read this and you know the secret — watch out!

Allen Brewster

About the Author

JOHN REYNOLDS GARDINER, an engineer who worked on the Space Shuttle, has also been employed as a writer for a television producer, and as an inventor for the Num Num Novelty Company, where he designed a plastic necktie filled with water and guppies.

A native of Los Angeles, Mr. Gardiner has travelled to twenty-nine countries and has lived in El Salvador, West Germany and Ireland. He and his wife, Gloria, currently reside in Huntington Beach, California, where Mr. Gardiner works as an engineer and gives seminars in writing for children.

Top Secret is Mr. Gardiner's second book. His first book, *Stone Fox,* was named an ALA Notable book.

About the Illustrator

MARC SIMONT was born in France and spent his early childhood in Barcelona. He studied art in Paris and New York. In 1954 Mr. Simont won the Caldecott Medal for *A Tree is Nice* by Janice May Udey. He has illustrated many other books for children, including *Mouse and Tim* and *How to Dig a Hole to the Other Side of the World*.

BANTAM SKYLARK BOOKS
A Reading Adventure

A stranger on earth needs Erik's help!

☐ **15694 THE FALLEN SPACEMAN Lee Harding $2.75**
Up above the earth a mysterious spaceship watches. One small
alien, tucked inside a huge spacesuit, is working outside the craft
when it suddenly blasts off. Poor Tyro alone and frightened, is
trapped on Earth. Luckily, it's Erik who finds him first.

Can there be such a thing as too much chocolate?

☐ **15639 THE CHOCOLATE TOUCH Patrick Skene
Catling $2.95**
John Midas loves chocolate more than anything else in the world.
Until the day he finds a funny coin, trades it for a box of chocolate
and—*the chocolate touch.* Suddenly, everything tastes like
chocolate and John finds out it's possible to get too much of a very
good thing.

Simon's new best friend is a ghost!

☐ **15622 GHOST IN MY SOUP Judi Miller $2.75**
Something funny is going on at Scott's house. Someone—or
something—is moving things around, stealing and making all
kinds of trouble which Scott gets blamed for. Only Scott knows
what's *really* going on, and who—or what—is to blame!

- -

Bantam Books, Dept. SK11, 414 East Golf Road, Des Plaines, IL 60016

Please send me the items I have checked above. I am enclosing $_____
(please add $2.00 to cover postage and handling). Send check or money
order, no cash or C.O.D.s please.

Mr/Ms _____

Address _____

City/State _____ Zip _____

SK11-11/89

Please allow four to six weeks for delivery.
Prices and availability subject to change without notice.

Wild and crazy adventures from
<u>Stephen Manes!</u>

☐ **BE A PERFECT PERSON IN
JUST THREE DAYS!**   15580-6 $3.25

Milo Crinkley tries to follow the loony instructions on being
perfect, found in a library book. But who ever heard of wearing
a stalk of broccoli around your neck for twenty-four hours? And
that's only the first day…

☐ **IT'S NEW! IT'S IMPROVED!
IT'S TERRIBLE!**   15682-9 $2.99

The TV commercials say the shoes that basketball star Ralph
"Helicopter" Jones wears are "New! IMPROVED! Amazing!
NEAT!" Arnold Schlemp just has to have them. At least until
the commercial steps out of his TV set and into his life!

☐ **CHICKEN TREK**   15716-7 $2.99

Oscar Noodleman spends his summer vacation entering the
"Chicken in the Bag" contest and eating 211 chicken meals at
restaurants across America! But Oscar's not the only one after
the $99,999.99 prize. Join the Chicken Trek!

Buy them at your local bookstore or use this page to order:

Magical Skylark  Adventures!

☐ **THE CASTLE IN THE ATTIC**
  by Elizabeth Winthrop   15601-2 $3.50

  William is sure there's something magical about the
  castle he receives as a present. When he picks up the tiny
  silver knight, it comes to life! Suddenly William is off on a
  fantastic quest to another land and time where a fiery
  dragon and an evil wizard are waiting to do battle...

☐ **THE GHOST WORE GRAY**
  by Bruce Coville   15610-1 $2.75

  Sixth grader Nina Tanleven and her best friend Chris are
  visiting an old country inn when suddenly the ghost of a
  young confederate soldier appears! They know he's trying
  to tell them something. But what?

☐ **THE GHOST IN THE THIRD ROW**
  by Bruce Coville   15646-2 $2.95

  For Nina Tanleven nothing is scarier than trying out for a
  part in the school play...except seeing a ghost sitting in the
  audience! Soon strange things begin to happen and it's up
  to Nina to solve the mystery!